Reactive

Helen Vivienne Fletcher

ISBN:

978-0-473-52061-8 (paperback)

978-0-473-52064-9 (mobi)

978-0-473-52063-2 (epub)

978-0-473-52062-5 (large print)

This one is for Rebecca.

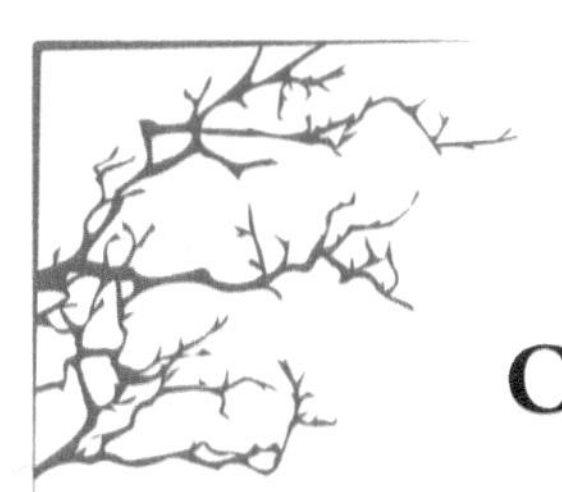

Chapter One

It was growing, that was for sure. Small green points crept up through the soil, spreading across the surface like a deformed octopus unfurling its tentacles. It was a succulent, but there was something different about it, something more sinister, like it had been crossed with a fungus, oozing poisonous sap.

Zo popped her head over my shoulder. "That is definitely not a sunflower." She laughed, sending brightly coloured sparks shooting out over me.

"Stop it!" I slapped my shoulder, as my jersey started to singe. That just made Zo laugh harder, spraying another round of red and gold embers.

"That's enough, Zoe. Back to your own work." Miss Trager's tone indicated this was non-negotiable.

Zo made a face at being called "Zoe" then turned back to her own plant spell. Naturally, she'd managed to grow a perfect yellow flower. In fact, looking around the classroom, I was the only one who hadn't produced something pretty and floral.

Miss Trager picked up my flowerpot. The stems were twisting now, turning a reddish-brown as they did. Miss Trager watched it, her lip curling in disgust. Her eyes didn't match the rest of her expression, though. The intensity of her stare and the way her breathing had deepened, she almost seemed excited... eager... Eager to use this to get me out of her class, probably.

Zo and Julianna's flowers were leaning out of their pots, their stalks curling around each other until the plants became one beautiful, exotic, living floral arrangement. I glanced down at my abhorrent creation and swallowed, my stomach churning. The leaves were starting to wilt, letting off an unpleasant smell.

"Oof, Toby let one rip!" Elijah yelled, causing an explosion of laughter from Asher and Julianna.

Fortunately, Zo kept a straight face. I wasn't sure I could take another fire. Miss Trager had told us Zo would probably start to develop magical manifestations – magistations as Zo called them – of all her emotions as time went on. We didn't know what they were going to look like, but let's just say I was planning to avoid getting her angry at all costs.

Miss Trager cleared her throat and the laughter stopped instantly. I wasn't sure if that was her using magic on us or just our fear of her severe gaze. Either way, the effect was impressive.

"Very... interesting, Toby." She craned her head to look up at me, still intimidating despite being a foot shorter than me. "I think Mr Grandace will want to see the direction your magic is taking."

The churning in my stomach went into double-time. Even after six months in this school, the headmaster's name still caused a knot of dread to form inside me, especially now Miss Trager wanted to show him my failure. She seemed to be waiting for a response, so I forced myself to nod, then shoved my hands in my pockets, and broke eye contact as soon as I could.

Miss Trager gestured for us to return to our desks. Like always, we clustered into the five desks in the centre of the room, finding security in being close to each other. It was weird. The classroom was set up for forty, but it had just been the five of us since the beginning. The whole school was like that – corridor after corridor but only our small group moving through them. Everything was really old too. Outside, ivy creepers wound over the school walls; inside, there were inkwells built into our wooden desks, and layers of names and other graffiti carved into the tops. I traced my finger over a pair of initials, surrounded by a heart. UT & AG, whoever they were, had left their mark. The staff claimed we were a pilot programme – the first class of our kind – but if that were true, the school had been here for sixty years waiting for us.

I leaned my chin on my hand, as Miss Trager began a lecture on the theory of botanical magic. I wasn't sure anything about my magic could be called botanical. The putrid stench still wafted from my flowerpot. Somehow, it managed to smell like both decomposing leaves and rotting meat.

I stared out the window over the school grounds and the rolling hills beyond them. Back home, I would have been furiously making notes every time a teacher opened their mouth, scared of failing a test if I missed something. Here, the tests were all magical, and I was pretty sure I was going to fail either way.

My gaze drifted to the open classroom door as someone walked past. My stomach dropped as I locked eyes with Mr Grandace, his black devil-beard and long flowing cloak as intimidating as ever. He held my eye for a moment then swept on. Two other staff members followed in his wake, quickening their pace to keep up with him.

There was a girl walking between them. She turned as she passed our room, her eyes meeting mine too. She had a wild look to her – her long dark hair loose and messy around her face, and she clutched a book to her chest, her fingers biting deep into it, as if it was by sheer force of will that she didn't implode.

She seemed to hold my stare for minutes, her gaze somehow both pleading and aggressive. Then she was whipped away.

I turned back to Miss Trager.

She frowned at me, the seriousness taking her well beyond her thirty years. "As you may have seen, you will have a new student joining you from tomorrow."

Elijah whispered something. I wasn't close enough to hear, but it sent up giggles from Julianna and Asher, and yet another round of embers from Zo.

"You will meet Calliope this evening after classes, for now please take out your grimoires."

We all groaned but pulled out our textbooks nonetheless, Elijah and Asher levitating theirs out, just to show off.

Zo leaned over to me. "You see her?"

I nodded. "Looked terrified."

Zo shrugged. "We probably all looked like that on our first day. She'll settle in."

Zo turned her attention back to Miss Trager, and I tried to follow suit. Something about the girl's stare haunted me though. I felt a crawling over my skin and I desperately didn't want to be sitting still.

A FAMILIAR TUG IN MY stomach told me when it was the end of classes for the day. Zo told me she saw the calls to move as streams of colours she had to follow, and Julianna had said something about a scent. For me, it was like a hand pulling at my belly button as if it would rip the remnants of my umbilical cord from my body if I didn't get up and go the way it wanted. The girls' versions sounded more pleasant, but either way, none of us were in any doubt when the school expected us to do something.

I walked back to the dorm room with Zo. She was trying to explain a spell to me, but all I could think about was my failed plant. Was it bad enough for me to get kicked out of the magic programme? The thought played on a loop in my head.

"Ow!" Zo jumped as she crossed one of the rune lines painted on the corridor floor, and a buzz of magic shot through her. "Dammit!" A clap of thunder sounded above us, and a rain of silver sparks fell over us.

I jolted too, stubbing my toe. "Ow, Zo!" I shielded my head as the deluge continued.

She laughed, and the sparks turned red and gold, before fizzling out. "Sorry, I got a fright."

I rolled my eyes. I guess that answered the question of what her scared-magistation looked like. I still wasn't looking forward to angry.

"Six months of crossing these things, and they still make you jump?" I kicked the rune line, feeling the magic tingle through my toes.

Zo poked her tongue out at me. "You jumped too."

I couldn't argue with that. We crossed over the next one and headed back to the dorm.

The new girl was already inside. She stood in the middle of the room still clutching her book. The wild look I'd seen in her had intensified, and I wondered if she'd heard Zo's thunderclap echoing through the halls. Her whole body was tight and alert, primed as if ready to run.

For a moment, we stared at her, then Zo took charge.

"Hey, I'm Zo."

The girl just stared back at us. She met Zo's eye, and her gaze was sharp, seeming to cut straight through. Zo hesitated, a flash of something that almost looked like fear crossing her face, then she pulled herself up taller.

"This is Toby." Zo jabbed me in the ribs, pushing me forward.

"H-hey." I wasn't sure whether it was the pain in my side from Zo's jab, or the girl's intense stare that made me stutter.

I reached out my hand to greet Calliope, but she looked at me as if she had no idea what I was doing. I froze, my hand still stretched out, then eventually, I dropped it to my side, stepping back. Fortunately, the others walked in at that moment, saving me from my own social incompetence.

Actually, it wasn't quite that simple. Julianna ran into the room, her eyes welling with unshed tears, and Asher followed after her, as if trying to scoop up and comfort a bolting toddler.

Elijah ambled in after them, smirking. I had no idea what was going on, but I was pretty sure I was already on Julianna's side. All three stopped dead as they saw us, a glance passing between them that seemed to be drawing up a contract of silence.

"This is Julianna," I mumbled. "And Elijah and Asher."

They muttered hellos, each more awkward than the last. Elijah disengaged quickly, moving to his bunk, but Julianna and Asher hung back, at least trying to look interested in the new girl. Not that Calliope looked interested in us. Her expression was still a cross between pissed off and terrified.

Zo sat down on the floor, perhaps trying to make herself look non-threatening. I took her lead, stepping back and leaning against the wall on the other side of the room.

"What's your name?" Zo asked.

The girl eyed us, then swallowed. "Calliope." Her voice was tight, but it was progress that we'd got her to speak.

"That's pretty." Zo smiled.

I just prayed Zo's rapport-building wouldn't result in laughter. Red and gold sparks were hardly going to put anyone at ease.

Zo pointed to the book in Calliope's hands. "I haven't read that one. Is it good?"

Calliope glanced down at the book, as if she'd forgotten it was there, though how she could while gripping it so tightly, I don't know.

She shrugged. "I just started. I was reading it for school."

Her hand was over the title, but the cover seemed vaguely familiar. I had a feeling the story had something to do with magic, not that it would help her here. Five minutes after learning magic was real, I learned everything I'd ever read about it was not.

"This will be your bunk." Zo pointed to the bed under mine. "If you ask nicely, Toby'll probably even let you have the top." Zo grinned at me.

Julianna had fought Zo desperately for the top bunk. Not that it really mattered. Each of the beds came with tent-like sides, so we could have our own space despite the fact that we were all sharing a single room.

Now that I thought about it, it was kind of weird we were in just the one room. The school was huge, but they'd crammed us all in here. Easier to keep an eye on us, I suppose.

Calliope crept forward, her eyes exploring the bed and the room. She pulled on the zip around her bed, experimenting with closing the sides.

"And you can put your stuff in here." Julianna indicated the chest of drawers at the end of our bunk. "I borrowed your drawers." She blushed. "But I'll clear them–"

"I don't have any stuff." Calliope cut Julianna off.

I frowned, suddenly noticing how little she was wearing. Not in a pervy way, just it wasn't warm, and the rest of us were all bundled up in two or three layers. Calliope wore a singlet, which was grubby around the neck, and a pair of ripped jeans. Goosebumps rose on her bare arms as I watched, as if to highlight how cold she must be.

"You don't have any other clothes with you?" Asher asked.

"What did I just say?" Calliope's voice was the loudest it had been since she got here, and the fear in her eyes was replaced by irritation.

"Sorry, I just meant–"

"Hey, don't worry about it," Julianna interrupted Asher's apology. "We can lend you some stuff, right, Zo?"

"Yeah, sure, of course." Zo gave a smile.

Calliope eyed them, seemingly wavering between suspicion and gratitude at the idea. "One of the teachers said they'd bring me some things," she said finally.

I was surprised Julianna had even made the offer. She was particular about her appearance, and I hadn't taken her for the sharing type. To be fair, I hadn't really taken much time to get to know her. Zo and I had become friends easily, but I always felt on the out with the others.

Julianna shrugged. "Well the offer stands if you need it."

There was something really off about this. Why had Calliope brought a book she was reading for school, but not bothered to pack anything else? The rest of us had arrived with a couple of suitcases each – admittedly, mine had been packed by my mum – but even Zo, who didn't seem to feel the cold and couldn't care less what she looked like, had brought a fair bit from home.

"I like your bracelets." Julianna reached out to touch Calliope's wrist.

Calliope jerked away. She clutched at one of the silver bands around her wrist, though it looked more like she was trying to pull it off than protect it. She had one on each wrist, and I saw the glint of another around her ankle through the rip in the hem of her jeans.

Julianna raised her hands, as if in surrender. "I'm sorry, I didn't mean to–"

Calliope shook her head, violently. "Is this a big joke to you people?!"

Julianna blinked, as lost as the rest of us. "What? I just said I liked–"

"Screw you!"

Julianna's cheeks flushed red. "What is your problem?!"

Calliope made a noise in her throat, looking away.

"I was just trying to be nice." Julianna shook her head. "You don't need to be such a–"

I stepped between her and Calliope automatically. Not that I really thought they were going to fight, but you could never be too careful with magic. Sometimes emotions running high led to some "interesting" accidents.

For a moment we all just stood there, Julianna glaring and Calliope looking determinedly in the other direction, then Calliope climbed into her bunk, pulling the zip closed, and shutting herself away.

There was an awkward pause, during which I realised Elijah had been watching the whole thing from his bunk, a stupid grin on his face.

"Well, that was weird." Zo cracked up, but Julianna still looked like she couldn't decide whether to yell or cry.

"It was certainly that." I lowered my voice, not wanting Calliope to hear and re-emerge to yell at us again.

Asher had crept forward and was standing awkwardly next to Julianna. I felt for the guy. With everyone else, he was Mr Confident, but around her, he got an attack of the shys. It didn't take a genius to work out why.

He cleared his throat and touched her back. "We should head down for dinner..."

"Yeah, I guess." Julianna's voice held on to the hurt, and she was still glaring at Calliope's closed sleeping pod.

Asher shifted his weight, perhaps trying to get Julianna to look at him. "You want to walk with me, Jules?"

Julianna blinked a couple of times, then nodded, a smile hinting at the corners of her mouth. I couldn't help it, but I smiled too. Call it cheesy, but deep down I had a soft spot for people falling for each other.

Elijah made a gagging noise. "Dude, do we have to watch this cutesy crap? Just jump her and get it over with."

Julianna and Asher's faces both flushed, and weirdly, so did Zo's. Her eyes flicked between Julianna and Asher, lingering more on Jules than him. I got the sense Zo's feelings for her weren't entirely platonic. I also knew her well enough to know she wouldn't want to talk about it.

"Yes. Food. Now," I said, trying to keep my tone light.

The others didn't need any more prompting. Zo and I both held back, letting them disappear down the corridor to the dining room. I fell into pace with her, then rubbed the top of her head, ruffling up her spiky hair.

"Don't!"

She squirmed away, then jumped, reaching up to try do the same to my hair. Being tall had its benefits.

"Ew, gel!" she said, as her hand finally connected with my head.

I laughed, smoothing my hair back into place. She unconsciously did the same, then nodded towards the dorm room, now we were out of earshot. "That came out of nowhere."

"Which bit?"

She gave a half-laugh, fortunately not enough to cause any fire hazards. "I meant the new girl. Good luck sleeping with her underneath you!"

I was tempted to make a dirty joke, but the truth was, the way Calliope had overreacted, I was a bit nervous about us sharing a bunk. Would she go off at me if I snored?

"She's new. She'll settle down." I wanted to believe that, but the way she'd looked at me when I first saw her in the corridor – the way she was clutching that book – she seemed scared more than anything else. I couldn't help wondering what of.

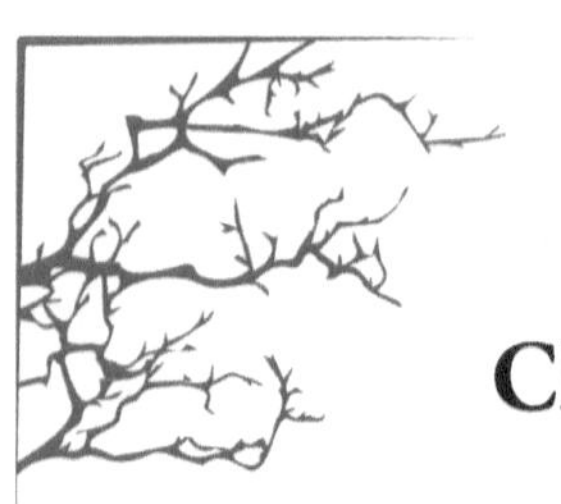

Chapter Two

Calliope did eventually join us for dinner, but only in that she came and sat down at the table with us. She didn't speak to anyone, and her hunched shoulders and prickly glare told us it wasn't because she was waiting for us to introduce the topic of conversation. Not that any of us were game to try now anyway. The air between her and Julianna was tense, and I was pretty sure we were expected to choose sides.

Things were still uncomfortable in the morning. I'd never been one for confrontation, so I skipped breakfast, heading down to the classroom early to avoid ending up in the middle of it.

Unfortunately, a bigger problem greeted me when I got there. My desk had been swallowed, a tangle of poisonous-looking foliage twisting its way around the metal and wood. It took me a moment to recognise the plant as my failed sunflower. The leaves had spread out, encompassing the pot and the tabletop, and tendrils cascaded to the floor. The whole thing was oozing, a red sticky liquid seeping down to a puddle on the Lino.

I stepped forward, torn between wanting to throw the whole thing out the window and a strange pride at having created something so impressively awful.

Weirdly, it didn't smell bad anymore. In fact, the sticky red liquid had a sweet, fruity smell. I was struck with an urge to touch it – to lick it. It reminded me of something... some food I'd tasted long ago and was suddenly desperate to try again. I found myself moving closer, reaching out a finger to...

I felt a little ping in my stomach, like an elastic band. It wasn't like the call from the school, it was something else. A warning, maybe. I took a step back, moving away from the sap.

"You won't be saying that when you see it!"

I ducked down behind the desk, as I heard Miss Trager's voice in the corridor. It was stupid, I was allowed to be in the classroom, but I still felt like I'd be in trouble for being in here alone.

Miss Trager and Mr Grandace's assistant, Miss Caraway, came into the room. I hid under the table, the creepers from my plant blocking me from view.

"Mr Grandace isn't convinced it's Toby."

My stomach lurched at the mention of my name.

"You're telling me this doesn't give you pause?" Miss Trager's voice was more animated than I'd ever heard it.

"Of course it does! But you know what the prophecy said: we keep them all safe, or we save none of them."

Save us? What were we in danger from? Things started to grind into place. We'd been brought here to learn, sought out and hand-picked for our latent magical ability... or so we'd been told. If we were really here because of a prophecy, it would explain why there were only six of us, and why my magical ability was hardly anything to write home about.

"But if the rest of it is true – if they really are a danger to humanity – then surely removing him would–"

"These are children, Ursula! One siren plant doesn't warrant 'removing' him."

I swallowed, squeezing myself in even tighter under the desk. It was pretty obvious "removing" me didn't mean sending me home. And what on earth was a siren plant? I edged away from the delicious-smelling sap, hoping the movement wouldn't alert the adults to my presence. The scent still tempted the back of my throat. I bit down on my lip, resisting the urge.

"I knew it was a mistake to bring them here. How do we know we haven't created a self-fulfilling prophecy by putting them together? They could have gone for years without meeting."

"Mr Grandace thought it was better to trigger them under our guidance."

Miss Trager made a noise in her throat. They both came closer, examining the plant above me.

"We'll have to move to another classroom," she said. "We can't expose them to this."

I felt a tug at my belly button, the magical pull telling me to move to the new room. I had to figure out how to get out from under here before I was discovered, or worse yet, got locked in here with my awful creation.

"I just... I don't want any more deaths on my hands." Miss Trager's voice was choked with emotion, and Miss Caraway was silent for a moment. She was the older of the two women, by decades, not just years, yet somehow Miss Trager was the one in authority. I wondered if my teacher was using magic to achieve that, compensation for her small stature and seemingly sweet face. She'd always scared the crap out of me, topped only by Mr Grandace.

"Please just promise me you won't act on this until we see how she influences him?" Miss Caraway said finally.

I guessed they must mean Calliope, but if she was our best bet for saving my magic, I wasn't sure there was much hope.

"I know the balance has been off, but she may be what we need to right this..." Miss Caraway trailed off at the sound of voices out in the corridor, the rest of my class following the magical call. She and Miss Trager stepped away from my plant, moving to the classroom door. I ducked out from under the table, scrambling across the room behind their backs.

I caught Zo's eye through the gap in the door and made a desperate face at her. She frowned, but quickly caught my meaning.

"Miss Trager," she said, darting forward and drawing both women's eyelines. "I was wondering if you could–"

Zo misjudged her leap forward and crashed into Calliope.

"What the hell?" Calliope glared at Zo.

It wasn't the distraction she'd intended, but it was the one I needed. I slipped through the still open door, joining the group as if I'd been walking with them the whole time.

"I'm so sorry!" Zo scrambled to pick up Calliope's books. "I really didn't mean to do that."

Calliope looked from Zo to me, and I could tell she'd seen exactly what happened. Her eyes narrowed, and for a moment, I thought she was going to blow everything. Then she shrugged.

"Look where you're walking, next time."

Zo widened her eyes at me, and I'm pretty sure that meant "you owe me". I made a face back that I hoped she knew meant "will explain later". At any rate, by the time Miss Trager glanced towards me, the classroom door was shut, and she had no idea I'd overheard anything.

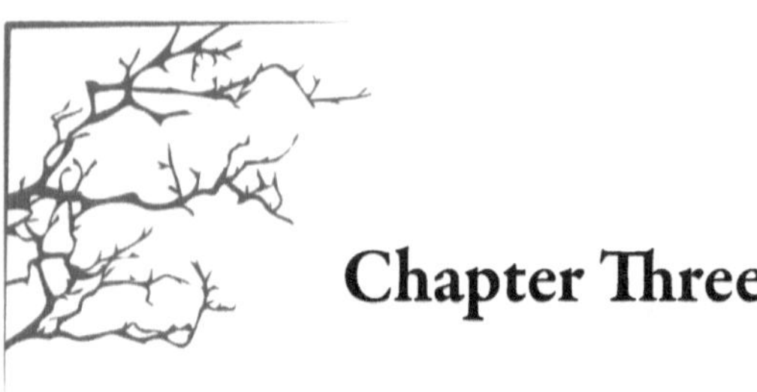

Chapter Three

I paid very little attention in any of my classes that day, doing even worse than normal. All I wanted was to talk to Zo. I was sure she would be able to help me make sense of it all.

In our last class of the day, Miss Trager said something that made me pay attention.

"All of you were especially chosen to come here…"

She avoided looking at me as she spoke, but I swore she was keeping an eye on me in her peripheral vision. Was she going to tell us about the prophecy?

"Each of you has a very special type of magic. You may have noticed your abilities have gotten stronger since you've been here."

That was hard to gauge, in my case. I hadn't known magic existed until Mr Grandace showed up at my home and insisted I needed to be trained in it. Perhaps that insistence should have been a warning sign.

"The six of you are each what we call geminus magic-wielders. That means your magic is twinned with another person's. Alone, you may struggle to control it – either it will fade completely as you grow older, or…" Miss Trager trailed off, swallowing as if unable to face what she'd been about to say.

Despite her fearful look, I allowed myself to feel a small amount of relief. Perhaps this is what she and Miss Caraway had meant about saving us. Alone, our magic could become dangerous, *a threat to humanity*. But when we were together, we would be able to gain control.

I'd seen the way Zo and Julianna's magic seemed to complement each other's; the way their work was stronger, more luminous, when they worked on spells together. Elijah and Asher weren't the working together type, but they were much further along in their magic than the rest of us and spent a fair bit of their time one-upping each other, in good-natured competition. It made them both work harder, and their magic had been gaining power because of it.

"This evening, I'd like you to explore working with your geminus pair. Julianna and Zoe, Asher and Elijah, I want you to work on finding the similarities in your magic. See where you can add strength to each other's spells, or correct areas where your partner's magic is going off course."

I could see where this was going. I made a face at Zo, and she shot me a sympathetic one back.

"Toby and Calliope..." Miss Trager paused again, her breath audible as she struggled with what to say next. "Just spend today learning more about each other."

So far, all I knew about Calliope was that she was weird and had anger issues. Well, that and she was apparently supposed to stop me becoming a threat to humanity. Probably not something I should lead with, but it sure sounded like us spending more time together was going to be worth everyone's while.

Miss Trager dismissed us, and I followed after Calliope, determined to start as soon as possible.

She didn't acknowledge me at first, keeping her head down and hiding behind her long hair. She was holding herself so tightly, she was almost vibrating. I fell into pace beside her, and stooped my head, trying to see if I could catch her eye. I couldn't.

"Can we try this again? I'm Toby." I held out my hand, but she didn't take it, nor did she break her stride.

"Callie," she said.

A nickname, that was something at least. I waited, but it became clear that was all she was going to give me.

"So, apparently our magic complements each other. Pretty crazy, huh?"

"I don't have any magic." Callie's voice was flat.

I let out a half laugh. "Well, you might be the lucky one then."

She frowned, and I realised she was serious. I cleared my throat. Laughing at her probably hadn't been my smoothest move.

"I thought that too when I first arrived." It had taken me and my parents a long time to believe that magic was even real, let alone that I had any. Mr Grandace had visited us six times before Dad finally let him in the door. Honestly, it was lucky Dad hadn't called the cops.

Callie shifted a little, looking up at me through her hair. I took that as encouragement and carried on.

"I'm not like these guys." I gestured to the empty corridor, indicating my absent classmates. "They all knew they had powers and could control them. Me? My magic was more... accidental."

"I don't have any magic," she repeated.

"Yeah, see you might think that, but sometimes it's kind of subtle. I mean, you wouldn't be here if you really had *no* magic, right?"

This time she just stared straight ahead. I felt my smile falter. Was I being patronising? I guess she would know better than anyone if she really didn't have any abilities.

"Sorry," I mumbled. The silence hung between us for a few minutes.

She sighed and stopped walking, turning towards me. "So, what does your magic look like then?" She fiddled with the bracelet around her wrist, not looking up at me, but her tone seemed genuinely interested, if a little reluctant.

"Like I said, it's always been mostly accidental. Things like, if I was scared, something would go flying off the table, or once, when I was excited, this tube of paint exploded all over the classroom at school." I guess I could see why Miss Trager was worried. I could probably do a lot of damage if my magic really went awry.

Callie's eyes flickered, and I could tell she was remembering something. No doubt she'd had something similar – an accident or strange occurrence she couldn't explain. It would make sense if our magic was supposed to be twinned.

I moved forward a bit, encouraged. "There was this one time where I got angry and all the electronics in the house turned on. We thought it was a power surge."

"Wow," Callie said – the biggest reaction I'd gotten from her about anything.

I relaxed a little at that. Strangely, I could tell that wasn't what she really wanted to say. It wasn't like I could read her thoughts – that had never been one of my magical abilities – but it was like I *knew*. She wanted to ask me why I was angry that day. Somehow, I was also certain that *she* knew I didn't want her to ask. Was this what the geminus connection was all about? I wasn't sure, but I decided to risk it.

"Anything like that ever happen to you?" I asked.

I held my breath as I waited for her to answer. She studied my face, her eyes flicking through a range of emotions. Then she turned away.

"No."

"Callie, please! This is important." Without thinking, I grabbed her arm.

She jerked away from me. "Don't touch me!"

"We need to control our magic. I need YOU to help control my magic. The fate of humanity could depend on it!"

Even as I said it, I knew it sounded insane. From the look on Callie's face, she was thinking exactly that.

She stepped back a pace, still staring at me. "I told you," she said, her voice low. "I don't have any magic."

For all I knew, I *was* crazy. I'd overheard half a conversation, and now I was trying to persuade a girl I barely knew she had to stop me from endangering humankind.

Callie turned and walked away, leaving me alone in the corridor.

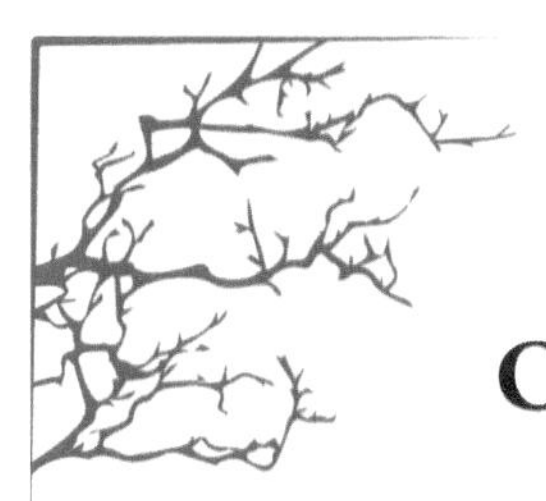

Chapter Four

Callie avoided me for the rest of the day, and honestly, I didn't blame her. I kept my distance, but I felt like I always knew where she was. I snuck looks at her, and every so often, I caught her looking back. It really seemed like she was feeling exactly the same thing I was.

I finally got to talk to Zo that night after the others had gone to bed. She climbed up onto my bunk, and I told her about the conversation I'd overheard.

"Woah," she said when I'd finished.

I didn't tell her what I'd said to Callie. I was too embarrassed, and I didn't want Zo waking everyone up by laughing too hard.

I'd been thinking about Miss Trager's words all day, but I still couldn't wrap my head around it. I wasn't even sure Zo would believe me, but she was my best shot. I could see it all running through her mind, but she didn't say anything else straight away. I waited as patiently as I could.

Finally, she took a breath. "What makes you so sure you're the danger?"

"What do you mean?"

"It sounds like they don't really know what this prophecy means. If one of us really is a *danger to humanity* – and that by itself is a big if – what makes you so sure it's you?"

I stared at her. Despite the time I'd spent puzzling over it all, it hadn't occurred to me to question that. "Well... Miss Trager seemed to think it's me."

"Yeah, but she doesn't *know*, right? I mean, my sparks are as likely to cause damage as your plant."

"No way. You'd never do something like that." I shook my head at the image of my vegetarian best friend hurting anyone.

Zo shrugged. "Not on purpose. But neither would you."

I couldn't fault her logic, but that seemed too simple an answer. She sighed, obviously realising I wasn't convinced.

"Take Asher, then. His magic is way stronger than both of ours put together. And Callie – we don't have a clue what's going on with her, and let's not forget Elijah. If anyone's likely to cause damage, it's that sociopath."

I frowned. "Sociopath? What?" Elijah was hardly the nicest guy, but did she really think he was that bad?

"Didn't you hear what happened yesterday? *His* plant – he grew these pretty flowers, then gave them to Jules. She was stoked until she broke out in a rash and started having trouble breathing. Turns out they're some poisonous, tropical thing. He did it for a laugh, called it a 'prank'. Didn't even care about how sick it made her."

"Wow." No wonder Julianna was crying when she came back to the dorm yesterday. That was a pretty awful – and dangerous – thing to do to someone.

"I mean, she's fine," Zo continued. "Asher healed her, no big deal, but Elijah's a jerk."

"Understatement." He was clearly a creep, though it still seemed a big leap from a nasty prank to causing danger to the entire world. Then again, it was an even bigger leap from my accidentally making a scary plant.

"I just mean, don't worry about it too much. If we really are in some kind of danger – whichever one of us is the cause – seems like we're in the right place for it, don't you think?"

It kind of freaked me out how calm she was being about it all. Normally, I loved how chilled out Zo was, but right now I felt like I needed more of a reaction. Knowing we'd been brought here under false pretences made me want to run. I mean, what else were they lying about? If it wasn't for the fact that it seemed like I'd be a bigger danger on my own, I would have been calling Mum and asking her to come get me. As it was, I just had to keep working on Callie, and hoping like anything I didn't kill us all in the meantime.

Zo yawned, and stretched, moving towards the ladder to climb down from my bunk. "It'll be okay, Toby. You'll see."

I wished I could be so sure. I watched her shuffle off to her bed, then I lay down – not that I really thought I was going to sleep.

A few minutes later, I felt a shift below me – Callie turning over in her sleep... or maybe not in her sleep. Was she awake? Had she been listening to everything we'd said?

It wasn't the end of the world if she had. Her taking the geminus thing a bit more seriously might work in my favour, but this wasn't exactly the best way for her to find out.

"Callie?" I whispered.

The sound of Elijah snoring from across the room was the only answer I got.

THINGS CONTINUED IN much the same way for the next week. Miss Trager treated me like normal, though since she hadn't liked me to begin with, that didn't say much. I didn't hear anything else about the prophecy, and I made no progress on getting Callie to work with me.

One strange thing I did discover was that Callie was getting up in the night. I never saw her do it, but twice I woke up to her creeping back into the room. The rational part of my brain told me she was just going to the bathroom, but if I'd learnt anything in the last few days, it was that rational didn't mean anything here.

Thursday night, I was lying awake, unable to sleep, when I felt the bed shift as Callie moved. I held my breath, not wanting her to realise I was awake. After a moment, I heard the soft sound of her feet padding across the floor, then there was a brief flash of light, as she cracked open the door and slipped out.

Again, the rational part of my mind told me not to follow. She already thought I was a creep. Stalking after her was hardly going to change her mind about that, but somehow, I couldn't leave it. I waited until I was sure she'd moved away from the doorway and then climbed down the ladder.

I padded down the corridors, looking for her. I quickly established she was not in the bathroom. But where was she?

I turned a corner, and there she was in front of me. I ducked back into a doorway, before she saw me, and hid in the shadows as she walked past.

She was muttering to herself, too softly for me to hear the words, and fiddling with her bracelet. I waited until she was a decent distance ahead, then crept after her.

She turned down another corridor. I wasn't sure where this one led. The school had so many twists and turns, it was hard to keep track of them all. But Callie was walking as if she knew exactly where she was going.

Suddenly, she stopped, staring down at something on the ground. She paused for a moment then did an about turn, heading back the way she'd come. I hid again, narrowly missing being seen, then watched as she turned down yet another corridor.

I crept to the corner, watching as she strode purposefully forward, only to stop abruptly after a few paces and turn back. Was it possible she was sleep walking? She looked wide awake, but her path made no sense.

I ducked back into a doorway as she came closer, but I wasn't quick enough this time. She rounded on me, glaring.

"What are you doing here?" She hissed.

"What are *you* doing here?" It wasn't my best comeback, but I thought the question was valid. She had no right to get angry at me for following her when she had no right to be here in the first place.

She glared at me, then turned away, continuing her purposeful, striding walk. I followed after her.

"Where are you going?"

She shook her head. "None of your business. Go back to bed." Suddenly, she stopped again, her eyes wide.

"What is it?"

Her fingers were spread, palms raised slightly, as if she'd seen something that frightened her. She swallowed slowly, then stepped backwards.

"Callie, what's wrong?"

She was shaking, staring at the floor. I followed her gaze, trying to work out what had frightened her. There was nothing there, except one of the painted rune lines which ran all over the castle.

I let out a breath as I realised that was it. "Hey, it's okay. You don't need to be scared of the runes. I know it feels weird when you cross them, but it's just protection magic."

She looked up at me, her face scrunching up. "Protection magic? Are you serious?" She spat the words at me

"Well... yeah." I stared at her, too baffled to know how else to respond.

She shook her head, the movement coming out jerky with anger. "You call that protection? What is the matter with you people?!" She turned, stalking back down the corridor.

"What on earth are you–?"

"Leave me alone!" she yelled over her shoulder.

At that point, that's exactly what I wanted to do – the girl had some serious issues – but then she turned the wrong way, heading towards the restricted staff area.

"Callie, wait, you can't go down there!"

I raced after her, expecting to have to chase her all the way down the corridor, but instead she was stopped at another rune line. She was teetering on her toes, as if she'd frozen suddenly, only seeing it at the last minute. I slowed my pace, walking towards her cautiously.

She let out a bitter laugh. "I bet you think this is really funny, don't you?" She sniffed, and I realised she was crying.

I reached out to touch her arm, but she flinched away.

"Honestly? I have no idea what to think about this. Why don't you go home if you hate it so much here?"

That wasn't what I wanted, of course it wasn't. She was the best hope I had of controlling my magic, but I was sick of having to act like a stalker just to get her to talk to me.

She took a sharp breath in. "Go home?!" Her face screwed up. "You're a jerk." She shoved past me, walking back towards the dorms.

I followed after her. "Jesus, Callie! I was just trying to help."

She rounded on me. "Help? You think trying to get me to cross those things is helping?" She flung her hand out, gesturing back at the rune line.

"So, it buzzes a little when you cross them? Why do you have to make such a big deal out of every little–"

"Buzzes?"

I shrugged. "Buzzes, tingles... I'm not sure what else to call it."

The anger had fallen from her face and now she was staring at me, a frown creeping down her forehead. She turned back, looking at the line. She shook her head, slowly. "You actually don't know, do you?"

I sighed, my patience with her well and truly gone. "Know what?"

"I can't..." She swallowed, audibly clearing her throat. "I can't cross the line, Toby."

"Huh?" It was the first time she'd used my name – the first time she'd used anyone's name as far as I could tell. I wasn't sure if that meant something, or if I was reading too much into it, but it felt significant.

She met my eye, holding it. She seemed so vulnerable, all of the bristle from the last few days dropping away. "I thought you all knew," she whispered.

"Knew what?" I repeated.

She stared at me. Everything seemed to slow down. I watched her blink, it seeming to take minutes for her eyelids to meet, then her lips parted, letting out a breath. She walked slowly back to the runes, stopping and looking at me as she reached them.

"I can't cross the line because of this..."

She took another step towards the rune line. Something pinged in my stomach. It was the sensation I'd felt when I was standing next to my plant. The sensation that had saved me from tasting the sap and from being caught by Miss Trager.

I grabbed Callie's arm, pulling her back.

"What are you–?"

"Shhh!" I clapped my hand over her mouth.

She moved as if to pull away, then her eyes went wide. I heard it too – footsteps, coming towards us. I pulled Callie towards the dorm, but she shook her head. There wasn't time. She grabbed my shoulders, forcing me down into a crouch behind a cupboard.

Miss Trager and Miss Caraway turned into our corridor. "Mr Grandace still says–"

"I don't care what he says! You've seen the oracles – there needs to be a sacrifice. I'm sure it's the boy." Miss Trager's voice was high and sharp, bordering on hysterical.

Callie glanced at me, and I pressed my finger to my lips.

"It's still not clear, Ursula. We can't–"

"We have to! As far as I can see, it's a given that he will die if his magic progresses. It's just a matter of how many others he takes with him."

I felt sick. Was it really that bad? My only options were to take myself out now, or kill god knows how many other people before dying myself anyway.

Callie was staring at me, but her face wasn't full of the horror I would have expected. Instead her expression was soft, sympathetic. She reached out, grasping my hand.

"Mr Grandace wants to give him and Calliope more time. He's sure she'll balance his magic."

Miss Trager made a noise in her throat. "Arthur doesn't know what he's talking about. That girl barely has enough magic to light a birthday candle." She sighed. "It's too late. We need to remove Toby, now."

I closed my eyes.

"We'll tell the other students he went home," she continued. "Don't worry about Arthur, I can handle him."

There was a pause, during which I swore I could hear Miss Caraway's conflicted thoughts battling it out.

"All right," she said finally. "But please promise me you'll make it painless."

Their footsteps continued towards us. In a second, they would be upon us, and I had no doubt us sneaking around at night would be exactly what Miss Trager needed to convince Miss Caraway neither of us were worth saving.

Callie squeezed my hand. I looked up as she stood. She gave me a half-smile, then stepped backwards, dropping my hand. I opened my mouth to tell her to stop, not to do whatever it was she was planning on doing, but she pressed a finger to her lips.

"Miss Trager!" she called, then she turned around, running straight across the rune line.

"Calliope, what are you doing?" Miss Trager yelled, but Callie didn't stop.

She turned back to look at me, for once the anger gone completely from her face. Instead she just looked sad, and at the same time kind of... proud.

The bracelets around her wrists snapped together forming shackles which bound her in place. A second pair around her ankles did the same.

I stifled a gasp. Miss Trager and Miss Caraway rushed towards her. A loud pop sounded, and suddenly the headmaster was in the corridor, standing next to them.

"What are you doing out of bed?" Miss Caraway asked.

Callie just stared at her. The two women were flustered, clearly wondering what, if anything, she had heard. Callie gave nothing away staring them down. It made sense now, why she'd got so mad when Julianna mentioned her bracelets, and why she'd spent so much time fidgeting with them.

Mr Grandace took hold of Callie's arm. "I think we'd better have a little chat." His tone was calm, but the deepness of his voice made me nervous. A flash of fear crossed Callie's face, then in another pop, they all disappeared.

I couldn't stop shaking. Callie was a prisoner here... Callie was a prisoner here, in this school, where two of the staff were trying to kill me, and she had just sacrificed herself to save me.

I leant back against the wall and covered my face with my hands. I'd asked Callie why she didn't go home if she didn't like it here, but I hadn't realised she didn't have the option of leaving. For the first time, I wondered if any of us did.

I SAT ON THE FLOOR for a long time. When Callie didn't reappear, I got up and made my way back to the dorm. I thought about waking Zo, but I wanted to talk to Callie before I brought another person into this. More than anything else, I wanted to know she was okay.

I could have gone looking for her, but where would I start? Besides, I had a feeling the rune lines were going to be difficult for me to cross now, even if I didn't have bracelets. Miss Trager had made it pretty clear she wanted me dead, so there was no way she was going to let me go wandering the school freely.

I lay awake listening to the others breathing. Elijah had a tendency to snore, and Zo sometimes let off sparks from her dreams, but otherwise it was usually pretty quiet in the dorm. Tonight, I was hearing every little creak and shuffle, wondering if it was Callie coming back, or worse, Miss Trager coming to "remove" me.

Finally, the dorm room door creaked open. Light flooded in from the corridor, but the others didn't wake. I froze, listening to the hushed voices outside the room, then Callie slipped inside.

I could see the silhouette of one of the teachers outside the door, so I didn't move, pretending to be asleep. Callie climbed into the bed below me, and the door closed, leaving us in darkness again.

I'd been desperate to talk to her, but now she was here, I felt nervous. Would she blame me for what happened? I still wasn't sure what *had* happened, let alone why.

"Toby?"

I let out a breath at her whisper. "Yeah, I'm awake."

I hung my head over the side of the bunk. She was sitting on her mattress, the blanket wrapped loosely around her. She looked really small in the middle of that space. The pyjamas she was wearing were too big for her, like half of the clothes they'd given her. Suddenly, it made sense why she'd arrived here with nothing but that book.

She bit her lip. "Can I come up?"

I'm embarrassed to admit, I blushed. This was not exactly what I pictured as the first time I had a girl in my bed. I nodded, awkwardly, and moved over to the wall. There was a rustling, then I heard her climbing up the ladder.

She brought the blanket with her, wearing it like a cape. She sat down cross-legged and wrapped it around herself.

"I'm sorry," I said. "I had no idea–"

She shook her head, brushing away the apology. "I couldn't let Miss Trager do that to you. I knew the headmaster would be called if I crossed the line. It seemed the simplest way to..." She shrugged.

The simplest way to stop them killing me. I reached out, touching her arm. "Thank you." I held her eye, wanting her to know exactly how seriously I meant that. She had quite literally saved my life.

She nodded, and I felt she did know. Just like when we'd talked earlier and I knew what she wanted to ask me, it felt like we were in sync.

"This is so stupid. Neither of us even have any magic!" I surprised myself saying that, but it was true. Since coming here, I'd only been able to produce the weakest of spells, or ones that went wrong, and I hadn't seen Callie do anything whatsoever.

Zo stirred in her sleep as my voice rose. Callie and I both froze as we waited for her breathing to return to normal.

"I know but try telling them that!" Callie whispered. She didn't specify who, but it was pretty clear she meant our murderous teachers. "We've got to get out of here."

"But how?"

"I have no idea. I've been trying since I arrived."

The madness of the situation really settled on me then. I had been here for six months, my biggest worry that I was going to fail exams. Meanwhile, Callie had been a prisoner.

"What happened to you?" I gestured to her wrists – to the bracelets bound around them. "How did you end up here?"

Callie shook her head. "Same as you, I'm guessing. Weird guy with a goatee kept showing up, telling my foster mum I have magical powers and that he was going to teach me. She thought he was high."

I gave a half laugh. "Yeah, my dad thought the same."

"But you eventually gave in?"

I nodded. I felt stupid about it now. I should have trusted my instincts. Something had seemed wrong about Mr Grandace from the start, but I'd gotten caught up in the idea of magic. We all had. Except Callie.

"I'm guessing you didn't?"

Callie shook her head. "No. We kept telling him to go away, but he kept coming back. He got more and more insistent, then eventually he grabbed me from school." Callie looked close to tears. "And my foster mum probably thinks I've run away. She's the nicest person I've ever lived with, but now…"

I wanted to tell her we would get her home, but I didn't know if I could promise that. I wanted to anyway – to force my-self to make it true.

Callie sniffed, staving off the tears. "I've been here for three weeks. They kept me isolated at first, then they put the bracelets on me before I joined the rest of you. Mr Grandace kept saying I was important – that the fate of humanity might depend on me being here."

I swallowed. "The prophecy."

Callie nodded. "I heard you and Zo talking about that. Honestly, I thought it was a trick to make me stay. I really thought you were all in on this."

I shook my head. "I'm sorry that happened to you." It seemed like such an inadequate response, but I didn't know what else to say.

"It's happening to all of us, Toby."

I wanted to look away – pretend I wasn't a prisoner here too – but I couldn't. Either our teachers were crazy, and we were all trapped here until someone figured that out, or… Callie squeezed my hand as if urging me on, though I hadn't spoken aloud.

Or we really were some magical threat to humanity.

"Either way, we have to stop it," Callie whispered, respond-ing to my unspoken thoughts.

"We will," I said. "I promise."

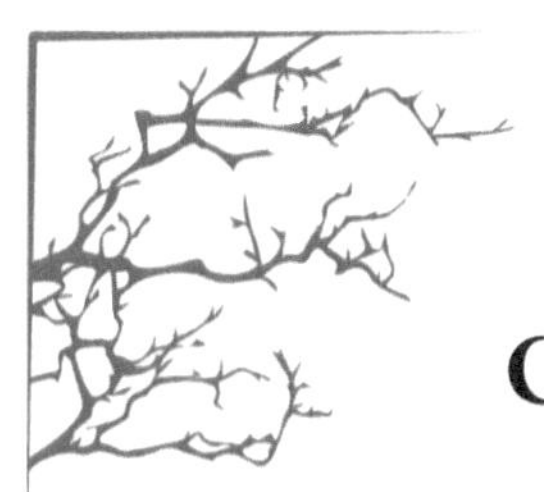

Chapter Five

Callie slept in my bed that night. Or rather, we both lay awake all night in my pod. We were too scared to be alone, but I'm not sure we were really any safer together. My magic would make a pretty useless defence if Miss Trager did come after us.

Callie climbed down before any of the others were up. I didn't think anyone had seen, until later that morning when Zo raised her eyebrows at me then glanced pointedly towards Callie. I wanted to tell her what had happened, but Julianna was having some kind of meltdown, and Zo was caught up in looking after her. Besides, Callie and I had agreed to try and act normal. If Miss Trager knew what was going on, we were sure she'd be even more determined to "remove" me.

Mr Grandace had told Callie he would be observing our classes for a few days, which seemed like it might offer us some protection, but I still felt uneasy as we walked down to our lessons. The call was pulling us outside, rather than into a classroom.

"Hey!" Zo prodded me in the back when I got to the sports field.

I jumped, more startled than I cared to admit.

She grinned. "What's going on with you and Callie?"

I stared at her, wondering where I could possibly start.

Her expression fell at my silence. "Are you okay, Tobes?"

I shook my head. "No, I don't think I am. I don't think any of us are."

Zo frowned. "Seriously, what's going on?"

I wanted to clue her in, but we needed to find somewhere private to do it. Miss Trager and Mr Grandace stood at the edge of the field. They were far enough away that they shouldn't have been able to hear, but I didn't doubt that they'd be listening in magically.

"Later," I said.

Miss Trager called us to attention and held up what looked like a normal dodgeball. "Being physically fit is just as important to your magical training as spells are."

I swallowed. She was staring at me, her gaze hard and intense. Normal dodgeball had been dangerous enough back home, let alone adding magic and a teacher who wanted me dead.

"You need to be able to focus your magic, even when under physical strain or mortal danger."

I frowned. This sounded more serious than dodgeball. I looked at Callie, but her eyes were fixed on the ball. She held herself tightly, as apprehensive as I was. I glanced around at the rest of the group. Julianna was hidden under a hoodie and sunglasses, still sulking about whatever happened this morning, though the rest were smiling, their eyes lit with excitement.

Miss Trager gave a sharp jerk of her hand and the ball burst into flame. Julianna gasped, but the others were laughing. Asher gave a whoop and high-fived Elijah.

Callie did meet my eye this time, and she looked like she was about to throw up.

"Make no mistake, children – this is real fire you are dealing with here," Miss Trager said.

There was something so perverse about her telling us it was real fire while calling us children. She tossed the ball lightly between her hands. It floated just above her skin, not burning her, but I could see her palms were red with the heat.

"Use whatever magic you have to keep the ball in the air and away from yourselves. Keep passing it, no matter what."

So, we were playing an extreme – potentially deadly – game of hot potato. I reached automatically for Callie, putting my arm around her. All I ended up doing was squeezing her, seeking the reassurance I couldn't give.

"She's going to kill us right now," she whispered.

I shook my head, but I couldn't quite find words to disagree with her. *We need to remove Toby...* Miss Trager's words repeated in my head. Callie stared over to where Mr Grandace was still watching. Would he help us if we told him? Would he even believe us?

"We need to run," I whispered.

Callie shook her head. "I can't. There are rune lines."

She was right – they were painted all around the field.

She squeezed my hand. "But you can. Go now, Toby."

"No." I was fairly certain I wouldn't be able to cross the lines either, but more than that, I couldn't leave her and Zo to deal with this alone. I was the reason for Miss Trager's anger, I couldn't let my friends get hurt because of it.

"All right." Miss Trager tossed the ball up in the air. It hung there, suspended like an artificial sun. "Everyone spread out. Zoe and Callie over this side, Toby and Julianna to the right."

Callie looked between me and Miss Trager. She was intentionally separating us. I felt a tug in my stomach, pulling me to move where Miss Trager had directed me to. Callie said she never felt the pull, but she was leaning away from me, the magic having its effect anyway.

"It will be okay," I said. It didn't sound comforting.

Callie nodded, releasing my hand like she was saying goodbye. She started walking away, hunching herself smaller as she did.

"Look after her, Zo." I stared at Zo, trying to make her understand the gravity of what was happening.

Zo frowned, as if she were about to protest.

"Please, Zo, she doesn't have any magic!"

Zo nodded. "True." Her confusion was obvious, but I trusted her to keep her word. "I'll do my best." She headed across the grass to join Callie.

Once we were all in position, the ball dropped. Asher dove forward, forgetting for a moment he couldn't touch it. Elijah shoved him out the way, pushing the ball up with magic instead.

They both laughed as it shot up, carving a golden arc across the sky. I held my breath. It was swooping down towards me. I raised my hands and widened my stance, hoping by some miracle I would be able to produce enough magic to send it flying away from me.

At the last second, the ball veered away, flying towards Julianna instead. She flicked her hand, raising a wind which sent the ball flying back at Elijah. She giggled, clearly pleased with herself.

Elijah sent it towards Callie this time. He was hitting it hard, sending the passes faster than they needed to be. Callie dropped back, and true to her word, Zo moved in front of her, keeping her safe. Zo was struggling with the force of Elijah's magic, though. She sent the ball away, but it wobbled, resisting her magic and still trying to follow the course Elijah had sent it on.

"Come on, Callie, at least try for the ball!" Miss Trager called.

I swear I could hear Callie swallow from across the field. She nodded, making an effort to look like she was getting ready to play.

Elijah had the ball again. He was spinning it above his head, showing off before passing it, then he shot it sideways, straight at Callie.

She threw her hand out, as if she was going to produce some magic, but at the last second she folded, ducking as the ball whizzed over her head. Even from where I stood, I could smell it had singed her hair.

Elijah cracked up, but he was the only one.

Asher shook his head. "Dude, chill. She hasn't got any magic."

Elijah's face darkened at Asher telling him off. Asher tossed the ball to Julianna. Zo was helping Callie to her feet, so Jules sent it back towards Elijah.

I could see it was a mistake before the ball left her hands. Elijah was pissed off, angry at us for spoiling his fun.

He swiped his hand in a sharp, striking blow. The ball flew off the field, towards Miss Trager and Mr Grandace.

Miss Trager shot the ball back at me. I dropped my stance, ready to fling it away but something was wrong. It was moving slowly, growing as it did.

"Toby!" Zo screamed, but it was too late.

The ball burst in mid-air, flames exploding over me. I saw Callie take two steps, running across the field, then she disappeared. Everything erupted in pain. I screamed, feeling myself burn.

"Oh my god, oh my god, oh my god."

Someone was repeating that, but I couldn't be sure who. Callie reappeared beside me and water blasted over us, drenching the flames. But I was still burning. I couldn't breathe. I stared up at Callie, gasping for air.

She stared back at me with panic written all over her face. Then she grabbed me, her fingers biting into my arms. She closed her eyes, scrunching them up. She started to glow, a warm light enveloping both of us. I closed my eyes too, letting it wash over me. The light tasted like honey, the sweetness filling my mouth and nose. There was nothing, nothing except the glow. And then slowly, it faded to black.

I WOKE, SUDDENLY. EVERYTHING was dark, and the pain had dulled to a throbbing ache. I shifted, trying to work out how badly I was injured.

"Shh, shh, shh."

I felt cool palms on my face, and I rested back against a pillow.

"Try not to move, you're still healing."

I opened my eyes. Zo sat next to my bed, her face pale in the dimly lit room.

"What happened?" My voice was croaky, and I tasted soot in my mouth.

Zo shifted, moving aside so I could see Callie asleep in the bed behind her. Callie's face and arms were bandaged. I tried to sit up, but Zo pushed me back.

"Hey... don't go undoing all her hard work."

I frowned at Zo, trying to piece together what I remembered.

She took pity on me. "She teleported across the field, conjured bucketloads of water, and healed your injuries. Pretty impressive for a girl with no magic."

"What happened to her?"

Zo sniffed. "She got burnt herself, before she put the fire out. Try as she might, she doesn't seem to be able to heal her own injuries."

She was hurt because of me. Was this what the prophecy had meant? Was this the type of harm I would cause to everyone around me? Maybe Miss Trager was right to try and get rid of me. I closed my eyes, letting the guilt wash over me.

I had pins and needles in my hand. I flexed it, trying to shake off the feeling. They continued, pricking at my fingertips. The sensation felt familiar, like the ping in my stomach. I sat up, reaching for Callie.

"What are you doing? You need to rest." Zo intercepted me, pushing me back.

"Please, Zo." I wasn't sure why it was so important, but I had to touch Callie's hand. I could feel the magic pulling at me, guiding me to reach over.

Zo stared at me. I could feel her confusion and doubt, but I also knew she trusted me. She gently lifted Callie's hand, without waking her, and placed it in mine.

I didn't know what I was doing, but I tried not to question it. The magic was flowing through me, running down my hand into hers. I watched as her wounds started to heal.

Zo gasped. "How did you...?"

I couldn't answer. Yesterday I could barely control my magic, and here I was healing Callie. It didn't make sense, but neither did any of what Callie had done to save me today.

Callie murmured, frowning in pain, then her eyes fluttered open. The magic moved between us, healing us. My pain eased, and colour came back into Callie's face.

"Woah," Zo whispered.

I wanted so much to explain it to her – warn her how much danger we were in, especially now Miss Trager had burnt me. But I could feel my eyes closing. Callie's eyelids were drooping too. She squeezed my hand as we both fell back asleep.

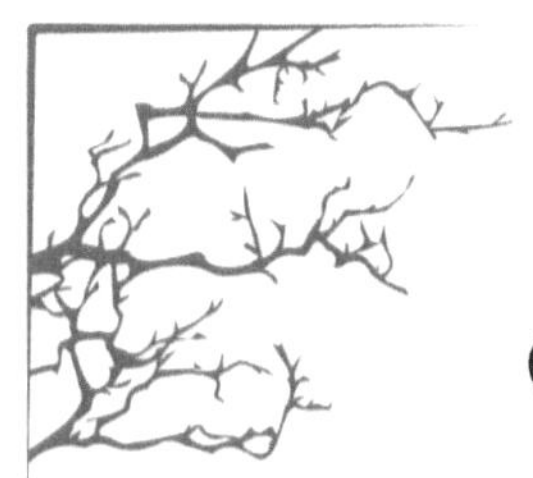

Chapter Six

When I woke again, Zo had left, and Callie sat on the edge of my bed, watching me sleep. Her bandages were gone.

"Finally," she said, as I opened my eyes.

I gave her a weak smile. She didn't speak again, the worry on her face saying it all. She jumped at a noise in the corridor, and I had a feeling she'd been doing that every few minutes while I slept.

The door opened, and I felt sick as Mr Grandace walked in. He sat down beside the bed, and Callie shifted, moving between us. She wasn't worried about herself, I realised. She was trying to protect me.

"How are you both doing?" Mr Grandace's gravelly voice made him even more intimidating. Neither Callie nor I spoke.

"I'm very sorry this happened to you. Accidents like this should never occur."

An accident? I couldn't tell if he was lying or just deluded.

"But the one good thing to come from it is we now know how your powers work, Calliope." His voice had a syrupy quality to it, and I was sure he was using magic to influence us. He smiled at Callie, and from her expression it was taking everything in her not to slap him.

I made a noise in my throat, and his gaze fell on me.

"Something you wanted to say, Toby?" His tone was genial, but his expression was not.

I almost lost my nerve, under his penetrating stare, but I couldn't just sit back and say nothing. "If I hadn't agreed to come, would I be a prisoner here too?" I gestured toward Callie's bracelets, giving away that I knew exactly what was going on. There was no more time for games and secrets.

Mr Grandace raised his eyebrows, and for a moment the surprise seemed to silence him. Then he shook his head. "Toby... there are forces here that you can't understand."

"So, explain it to me."

Mr Grandace sighed and leaned back in his chair. He stared at me and scratched at his devil-beard. This was the first time I'd ever seen him look unsure of anything. "This is much more complex than just you and Callie."

I stayed silent. He wasn't going to get off that easy.

"There are prophecies. You are both more important than you realise."

He paused. I waited for more of an explanation, but the silence stretched out.

"Really? That's all you're going to give us? We already heard about the prophecy from Miss Trager. Before she tried to kill us."

Mr Grandace blinked, and in that moment, I could tell he'd really thought the fireball was an accident. It didn't make me trust him any more than I had a minute ago.

He cleared his throat. "You and Callie both have a very special type of magic," he said carefully.

Callie sighed. "We're geminus. We know."

Mr Grandace shook his head. "No, your classmates are geminus pairs. The two of you, you're something... more." He stood, pacing the room in a forced way.

This was new, but how could we be sure he was telling the truth?

"Reciprocus magicae – reactive magic. Basically, your magic will respond to the situation – react to it – in whatever way it sees fit, with or without your approval."

Like Callie suddenly being able to teleport and me being able to heal her. I frowned. That didn't sound like such a bad thing, but Mr Grandace's tone implied it was.

"It's rare for magic users to be both twinned and reactive. It is a somewhat... volatile combination."

Callie and I glanced at each other. We had both shown magic well beyond our abilities in the last 24 hours, but I couldn't see how that justified trying to kill me.

"Now that your magic has activated, Callie, my hope is that your connection will allow you to influence each other's magic. The prophecy warned of very dire consequences if your magic is not controlled, so you can understand why we have gone to..." he gestured to Callie's bracelets, "such measures to keep the six of you here. But please know, I do not in any way condone Miss Trager's actions here today. Rest assured she will be reprimanded."

With a slap on the wrist, no doubt. Even if she did get what she deserved, that wouldn't solve anything. It was my fault Callie was being kept prisoner here. Mine, and our reactive magic.

"I do accept that this is hard for you both, and I'd like to try to make it a little easier. I understand you've been feeling confined, Callie." Mr Grandace was using that syrupy voice again, and a wave of turquoise floated out from him.

Callie blinked, slowly. I was struck by how restrained she'd been in dealing with the staff who were keeping her prisoner. The colour surrounded her until it seemed like she was breathing it. It had to be a spell, that much was obvious, but for what? I wanted to pull her away from the cloud, but I had a feeling I wasn't supposed to be able to see it.

"I'd like to give you some more freedom."

Hope flickered in her eyes, but she shut it down. I hated seeing that – the way she couldn't let herself feel happy.

"I realise you'd like to be able to explore a little more. From now on, you may cross the rune lines as long as Toby is with you." Mr Grandace let out another wave of colour – purple this time.

Callie's eyes took on a glazed look. He was trying to control her – make her think this was a good idea. I squeezed her hand, wanting to shake her free of it. Some of the colour dissipated as I did. She blinked, the influence seeming to clear, then frowned, and I felt my forehead pucker up too.

She looked from me to Mr Grandace. "So, basically you're making him my jailer?"

My stomach turned when she put it like that. It was sick enough that they were keeping her here, now they were making me a part of it. I dropped her hand, not wanting her to feel in any way restrained by me. How could the staff here possibly think this was okay? Without thinking, my hands were in fists, the anger rising in me, needing an outlet.

Mr Grandace raised his eyebrow and sniffed, his frustration obvious. "Our estimate is that the events mentioned in the prophecy will begin sometime in the next few days. One way or another, this will all be over very soon."

Callie looked away, blinking hard, then she took a breath and turned back to him. "Thank you. I'm sure Toby and I will make great use of the extra *freedom*."

I itched to get up and walk away – or better yet to punch him square in the jaw – but Callie's face was calm, waiting patiently for him to leave.

He sighed. "With time I hope you will both come to understand this is the best thing for everyone." He stared at us for a moment, before turning away and leaving us.

I couldn't look at Callie. She must hate me for causing all this. I hated myself for it. But as soon as Mr Grandace was gone, she turned to me, leaning in close to whisper.

"Tonight, Toby. You and I are getting out of here."

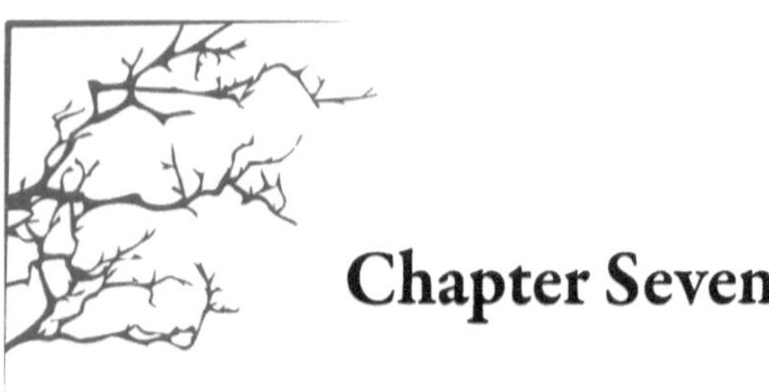

Chapter Seven

There wasn't time to tell Zo we were leaving. Callie convinced me the safest thing would be to get ourselves out, and then send help for the others. She was right – if I really was a danger to everyone, then getting as far away as I could was the best course of action. It still felt like a betrayal to leave without Zo. Not to mention the fact that I was putting Callie in danger by staying with her. I'd already been the cause of her imprisonment and left her with burns. As soon as she and the others were somewhere safe, I would get myself as far away as possible from everyone.

We waited until curfew passed, the school's lights going out for the night, and then snuck out of the nurse's office. I just hoped Mr Grandace had been true to his word about letting Callie cross the rune lines if I was with her.

We paused when we reached the first one. I looked at her and she shrugged.

"Guess there's only one way to find out." She stepped across it.

I held my breath, but nothing happened. I grinned and followed her. "Come on, we better keep moving."

We raced down the hallway, towards the staircase, but the door to the stairwell was closed. This was a bad sign; it had never been shut before. I rattled the doorknob anyway, hoping against hope it would be unlocked, or that I could break it.

"We're trapped." Callie's eyes were wide, and I could feel mine mirroring hers. I half expected our reactive magic to appear then, showing us another way out, but no such luck. If we couldn't get to the stairs, we would be stuck here. Unless...

"This way," I whispered.

Miss Trager would have locked all the doors, but there was a chance the windows would be unlocked. The temporary classroom we'd used after my plant took over had an oak tree right outside. I grabbed Callie's hand, taking off at a run.

We crossed two more rune lines on the way to the classroom. They no longer shackled Callie, but I had no doubt they would be tipping someone off to our movements.

I opened the window in the classroom. The branches weren't as close as I'd imagined them. We would have to jump. I climbed up onto the sill.

"You can't be serious!" Callie stepped back from the window, her eyes wide. A wild wind blew, sweeping the limbs of the tree close to us, then violently away again.

"Do you have a better idea?"

She chewed on her lip, her fear obvious, then eventually shook her head.

I reached for a branch. It was just beyond my fingertips, the wind battering it back and forth. I waited until a gust threw it towards me, then jumped, letting myself fall. Callie screamed as I did, but the momentum flung me far enough to grasp the tree. I swung forward, finding my footing on a branch below.

"It's okay, Callie. I'm okay," I said as soon as I had enough breath.

She was shaking, her face pale. "I thought..." She shook her head.

"Your turn." I reached out my hands. She wouldn't have to fall; I could pull her across, but I could see how scared she was. "I won't drop you, I promise."

Her mouth pressed into a firm line, and she nodded, once. We reached out, our hands locking.

"Now jump," I said, but she already was. I pulled her across, aiming for the branch below me. Her feet found it, and she let go of my hands, dropping into a crouch to gain her balance. She looked up at me, sweat slicking her grinning face.

Then the branch snapped beneath her feet.

"Callie!" I lunged forward, grabbing for her as she screamed. My fingertips grazed her palm, but still she fell.

"No!" I threw my hand out again, clasping for her. She froze in the air. My hand was nowhere near her, my magic having caught her instead. She stared at me, her mouth and eyes wide, still caught in the feeling of falling. I kept my hand where it was, palm up, fingers spread, too scared of disrupting whatever it was that was holding her to move.

I let out a little nervous laugh, but the panic on Callie's face wasn't easing.

"Toby," she whispered.

It was then that I noticed there was no branch beneath my feet either. Callie's hand was spread out like mine. I had saved her, suspending her in the air, but now she was suspending me too, both of us dangling there dependent on each other.

I swallowed. "We need to get down."

Callie nodded, beads of sweat appearing on her forehead again. "How?"

That was the question, wasn't it? How did we set each other down without dropping ourselves?

"Close your hand into a fist," I said. It might mean she dropped me, but maybe I'd be able to keep her afloat long enough as I fell.

Callie shook her head. "I'm not dropping you. *You* close *your* fist."

I laughed, not because it was funny but because we were as stubborn as each other. "Same time?"

Callie gave a single nod. We didn't need to count to three, I could sense her thoughts, our bodies moving in sync. We closed our hands, and both dropped to the ground with a whoosh.

Somehow, she landed on top of me, knocking the air out of me.

"Toby? Toby are you okay?" Callie shook me, but I didn't have the air to answer yet. We'd hit the ground hard, but it was soft and wet, the mud cushioning our fall. Apart from being winded, I was fine.

"Toby!" Callie's voice was high-pitched with panic, and I forced a spluttering cough out.

"I'm fine, I'm fine. Are you?"

She nodded, pulling me into a hug. "How did you do that?"

I hugged her back, though it hurt where she squeezed my chest. "Hey, you save me, I save you, right?"

I felt a ping in my stomach again, this time harder than the others had been. I pulled back to look at her. "You save me, I save you..." I repeated. That's what the prophecy meant. I don't know how I could possibly know that, especially as I'd never heard exactly what it said, but suddenly I was sure of it.

Callie stared at me blankly, unable to hear me over the wind.

"We have to go back," I shouted.

"What? No, we just got out of there." Callie stared at me like she thought I'd hit my head.

The pings in my stomach grew, firing again and again, like fireflies were dancing around in there. I turned towards the school, and it became even more insistent.

"We can't! Miss Trager will…" Callie trailed off. Her eyes darted back and forth, her mouth dropping open. "Fireflies," she said.

It couldn't be a coincidence that she'd said that right after I'd been thinking about them.

"Where?"

Callie pointed. "A trail of them." She traced the pattern in the air, leading around the side of the school.

"We have to follow them."

"We can't," she whispered. She stared at me, her eyes filling, and her forehead broken by a frown.

This would be our only chance of escape; we both knew that. But we could feel the pull of our magic, asking us to return. It wasn't like the school's calls. We could resist it if we wanted to. But our magic was reacting to something, and it wanted us to follow.

Callie blinked, and the tears fell from her eyes. "Okay," she whispered. "Let's go." She linked her arm through mine, bracing us against the wind, and led me the way the fireflies indicated.

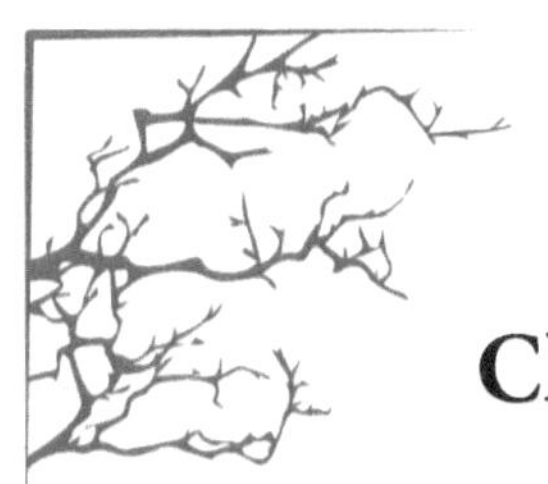

Chapter Eight

The trail led us back to our regular classroom, or rather, what had once been our classroom. The windows were blown out, the twisting tentacles of my plant forcing their way through.

"What the hell is that?" Callie yelled over the wind.

I shook my head. "It's me."

She frowned, not understanding, but there wasn't time to explain. Around the horrific monstrosity I'd created, I could see sparks flying, and there were screams coming from inside. Zo was in there.

"Come on."

Callie trailed after me. "How are we going to get back in?"

I slowed my pace. We were locked out. All of Miss Trager's attempts to keep us inside had failed but were now backfiring in a bizarre way. I turned back toward the classroom. The wall bulged with the weight of my plant, a large crack appearing in it. "I don't think it's going to be a problem."

The ground outside was soft, waterlogged, like the earth under the tree had been. Strange, as it hadn't been raining. We slipped as we made our way over to the wall, and we had to duck as more of Zo's sparks flew out at us.

"Cover your mouth and nose. Don't let the smell draw you in." I ripped the bottom off my shirt, wrapping it around my face. Callie did the same.

We squeezed through the crack in the wall, taking in the scene inside. My plant was huge, encompassing most of the room now. The sticky sap covered the floor, but water was rising, seeping up through the ground and creating a sweet-scented deluge. Even through the fabric, I could smell it, drawing me in.

I felt the ping in my stomach and stepped back.

"Ow!" Callie accidentally brushed against the plant, then flinched away. She raised her arm, inspecting the wound. There was a bright red rash appearing on her skin.

I glanced at the plant. Small, tropical flowers peeked out between the tentacles. My plant had mixed with Elijah's poisonous one.

"Toby!"

I recognised Julianna's voice coming from somewhere in the room. Callie and I edged our way around the side of the plant to reach her. We found her on the other side. She was clinging to Miss Caraway and Mr Grandace's wrists, desperately trying to hold them back. Asher had his arms wrapped around Elijah, struggling to keep control of him. Their eyes were glazed and they pulled away from Julianna and Asher, blindly trying to reach the plant.

"It swallowed Zo and Miss Trager already!" Asher yelled.

I looked up. The shooting sparks showed Zo was still alive but for how much longer? The sparks weren't just around her anymore, either. Leaves lit up with them, letting off charges of their own. Miss Caraway broke away from Julianna.

"No!" Julianna lunged to grab her again, but in the process lost control of Mr Grandace too.

I watched, horrified, as both of them disappeared into the tangle of plant limbs.

"Why didn't you stop them?!" Julianna screamed.

That was a good question. Why didn't I? I felt lightheaded. I glanced at Callie, and noticed she was swaying slightly, the siren sap pulling her in. The fabric covering our faces wasn't working. It took the edge off it, but we were still being drawn.

I shook my head to clear it. I grabbed a piece of broken glass and slashed at the plant, cutting off a stalk. The remaining tentacle drew back, as if avoiding my blade, but then layers of bark grew over it, instantly healing itself.

"No use," Asher yelled. "We've thrown everything at it, but it keeps healing and drawing more people in."

"Why isn't it affecting you two?"

"It can't." Asher sniffed. "I've got barely any sense of smell."

Julianna made a noise in her throat and pulled her hoodie back from her face. Her skin was warped, extra layers growing across her nose and one of her eyes. "Your healing spell worked too well," she said to Asher. "The skin won't stop re-growing."

I stared, horrified, and so did Asher. That was awful, but it worked in our favour right now. Callie swayed towards the plant again, and Julianna grabbed her, holding her back.

"I'm fine, it's okay." Callie slapped herself across the face, trying to regain control, but her eyes were still glazed, and Julianna's grip on her was waning.

"Find something to tie yourselves together," I yelled to Julianna.

My eye landed on Callie's bracelets. Before the thought even fully formed in my mind, our magic was reacting. The bracelets twisted, shackling Julianna and Callie together. That would hold her back at least.

Elijah was mumbling now, talking about how hungry he was and needing to taste the sap.

"Dude, help me!" Asher called.

I grabbed Elijah's arms, helping Asher force him back. It was hard with the wet floor; my feet slid underneath me. A gust of wind rushed through the room, swooshing through the branches of the plant, making them claw over us like reaching hands. My back burned as it connected with poisonous flowers and sparking leaves.

Wind... Like Julianna used during the fireball game. I looked around at everything that was happening. The plant was mine, but it had parts of the others in it – Elijah's poisonous flowers and Zo's sparks. It was healing itself excessively, like Asher's spell had done to Julianna, and I guessed the water was coming from when Callie had put the fire out. There was a piece of each of us in there.

"I save you, you save me," I whispered.

Suddenly, I could feel it, like I had when I first found the connection with Callie. The ping resounded six times inside me. Our magic wasn't twinned, it was the six of us – *all* of our magic linked. Without each of us controlling it, we would destroy everything.

The pings inside me were arrows. I knew what I had to do. I leaned back, spreading my arms wide, letting the magic flow from me. It shot out, spreading lines between us. I felt as each one hit one of my classmates.

Elijah resisted at first. I could sense his thoughts. How awkward and angry he felt all the time; how he just wanted to let go, let the plant take him. Suddenly, I could sense everyone's thoughts. They each sent their own call back, our magic linking and communicating between us.

"What the hell was that?" Callie asked. The glazed look was gone from her eyes, and she glowed with the magic flowing through her. We were all glowing.

"We're all reactive," I said. I didn't know if they would understand, but I felt it. We had to let the magic take over.

Julianna was the first to start. Her wind, which had been blowing the limbs of the plant around, allowing it further reach, changed direction, blowing the scent away from us. Elijah's thoughts cleared as soon as it did.

He drew out his poisonous flowers, directing them down into Callie's water. They poisoned my plant's and its own life source, the magic keeping itself in check. Meanwhile, Asher's healing turned to us, ridding the poison and siren sap from our bodies.

As the plant began to wither, Zo appeared at the top of it, standing strong as if the leaves had created a platform for her. Her and Callie's powers wrapped themselves around each other. The water cooled the sparks, and the sparks dried up the water, somehow both of them exactly in sync, both reducing each other, neither taking over.

And me? I remembered what Miss Trager had said. There had to be a sacrifice. I turned and walked straight into the centre of the plant.

MR GRANDACE, MISS CARAWAY and Miss Trager were all in the centre, limbs restrained by creepers, and a cage of branches surrounding them.

"I see now what you were trying to do," I said, though whether to my magic or my plant I wasn't sure. "You knew they were trying to hurt me".

Miss Trager shook her head, desperately trying to deny it, but it was no use. I knew it all now.

"The six of us are strong now. We are balanced."

Miss Trager and Miss Caraway stared at me, bug-eyed in panic. But Mr Grandace had taken on a calmness. He understood. They hadn't factored themselves into the prophecy. The six of us were never destined to be a danger. It had been their interference which had caused the problems, bringing us together before we were supposed to meet, and then trying to remove me from the group.

Our magic was strong, and it belonged to all six of us equally. One of us trying to use it would always fail. The sacrifice was not my death, but the deaths of all of us. There was no Toby now, nor Zo, Callie or any of the others. We were all one.

We smiled, a sudden peace rushing through all of us. We were terrifying, capable of destroying humanity, just as Miss Trager had predicted. We were also capable of saving it.

"Be a sunflower," I said to my plant, and I felt all five of my classmates repeat it softly with me. "Be a sunflower."

In an instant, my plant – Elijah's plant, the wind, sparks, water and all the rest of it – was gone. Instead, in Miss Trager's hands was the sunflower she had asked for.

Enjoyed this book? You can make a big difference.

REVIEWS ARE THE MOST powerful tool when it comes to getting attention for my books.

As an indie author, it can be hard to get my books into the hands of readers, but honest reviews help me do just that.

If you've enjoyed this book, I would be very grateful if you could spend just a few minutes leaving a review (it can be as short as you like).

Thank you very much!

Also by Helen...

WE ALL FALL

Myra fell from the trapeze, and then she fell in love. Which one will hurt her the most?

Something is not right at the circus. Since Myra's accident, there have been an unexplainable number of falls, and a strange, hot wind whispering through the tents.

Then, a new fortune teller arrives.

Myra meets Giselle, the beautiful, blind, child fortune teller, who often speaks of spirits in a way which may or may not be a joke. Myra finds herself drawn to her, despite the fact that she doesn't believe in psychics.

When someone she cares about becomes the next victim of the falls, Myra must face the unnatural cause behind them. Will Myra be able to save the people she loves, or will she be the next one to drop?

BROKEN SILENCE

A stranger just put Kelsey's boyfriend in a coma. The worst part? She asked him to do it.

Seventeen-year-old Kelsey is dealing with a lot – an abusive boyfriend, a gravely ill mother, an absent father, and a confusing new love interest. After her boyfriend attacks her in public, a stranger on the end of the phone line offers to help. Kelsey pays little attention to his words, but the caller is deadly serious. Suddenly the people Kelsey loves are in danger, and only Kelsey knows it. Will Kelsey discover the identity of the caller before it's too late?

UNDERWATER

Bailey has a lot of secrets, and a lot of scars, both of which she'd like to keep hidden. Unfortunately, Pine Hills Resort isn't the kind of place where anyone can keep anything hidden for long.

When Bailey arrives, she just wants to get through summer quietly, spending as much time in the water as she can.

Then she meets Adam.

Bailey's not looking to make friends, but Adam isn't easy to ignore. Neither is his ex-girlfriend, Clare.

As Bailey grows closer to Adam, she draws Clare's animosity. Will Bailey be able to keep her past a secret, or will Clare discover and reveal the sinister truth about how Bailey really got her scars?

SYMBOLIC DEATH

A woman finds a Death Curse symbol scratched into the soap scum around her sink.

A young boy watches his family fall apart after the death of his father.

A butterfly chrysalis hatches under the watchful eye of a hungry cat, and a teenage grim reaper's job is made harder by the boy who can see her.

Symbolic Death is a collection of sad, poignant, and darkly funny tales about death. If you like unique points of view, heartbreaking moments, and a touch of black humour, then you'll love Helen's short story collection.

Buy the ebook or paperback now or get it for free by joining Helen's mailing list at www.helenvfletcher.com.

About the Author

Helen Vivienne Fletcher is a children's and young adult author, spoken word poet and award-winning playwright. She has won and been shortlisted for numerous writing competitions including winning the Outstanding New Playwright Award at the Wellington Theatre Awards, making the shortlist for the Story-lines Joy Cowley Award, and the finalist list for the Ngaio Marsh Best First Book Award.

Helen has worked in many jobs, doing everything from theatre stage management to phone counselling. She discovered her passion for writing for young people while working as a youth support worker, and now helps children find their own passion for storytelling through her work as a creative writing tutor.

She lives in Wellington with her disability assistance dog, Bindi – a five-year-old, playful Labrador who loves soft toys, cuddles, and can fit three tennis balls in her mouth at once.

Overall, Helen just loves telling stories and is always excited when people want to read or hear them.

Read more at https://www.helenvfletcher.com/.